The
Magic Bottle

Other brilliant stories to collect:

The Magic Bottle

Retold by
Pat O'Shea

Illustrated by
Steve Lavis

SCHOLASTIC
Home of the Story

Scholastic Children's Books,
Commonwealth House, 1–19 New Oxford Street,
London WC1A 1NU, UK
a division of Scholastic Ltd
London ~ New York ~ Toronto ~ Sydney ~ Auckland
Mexico City ~ New Delhi ~ Hong Kong

First published by Scholastic Ltd, 1999

Text copyright © Pat O'Shea, 1999
Illustrations © Steve Lavis, 1999

ISBN 0 590 11350 X

Printed by Cox and Wyman Ltd, Reading, Berks.

4 6 8 10 9 7 5 3

The right of Pat O'Shea and Steve Lavis to be identified as the author
and illustrator respectively of this work has been asserted by them in
accordance with the Copyright, Designs and Patents Act, 1988.

For my dearest granddaughter Rosie —
with all my love.

In a time gone by there lived a small family – a father, a mother and two very young children – in a little cottage in Ireland. They were very poor for they had to get their living from what they could manage out of two small fields. In one of the fields the father grew potatoes, cabbages, carrots and onions;

and in the other field the mother had her four hens, the cow and the pig.

Sometimes they all had just enough to eat, other times they had not quite enough to eat; but they never ever had too much to eat. Potatoes were their main food and some always had to be set aside for the pig and the hens and some as seed to grow next year's crop.

The father's name was Mick Purcell and the mother was called Molly and the little children were named Billy and, I think, Ellen. They were all healthy and happy and they loved their simple home.

People in those days used to say that a pig was "the gent that paid the rent" – because when the pig was well-fattened he would be taken to market and sold. Not only was there always enough money to pay the rent but there was also enough to buy a tiny piglet to bring home to begin the process all over again.

Then one year without warning, disaster struck. The new crop of potatoes rotted in the ground, the cabbages were gobbled up almost overnight by a plague of starving hairy caterpillars, and the carrots and onions got some kind of wasting disease that first of all made them go all puny and then caused them to just wilt away. Worst of all, the pig got the head-staggers and the hens got the pip – and then they all died, poor things!

The little children were very upset about the pig and the hens, for the pig

was an amiable and charming creature who always allowed them to have a ride on his back, where they could pretend that he was a very fine horse even though he smelled peculiar; and with the hens gone, there was nothing left to chase around the place for fun and no more eggs. But of course, that was not the worst of it. Where could they get money?

"We are in terrible trouble now with the rent almost due," said the father. "Something must be done!"

"We need a miracle," the mother said.

"We'll have to sell the cow," said the father.

"Away you go, Mick, and do it; and be very sure to get a good price for her," said his wife, making up her mind at once.

At this, little Billy and Ellen burst into tears, not only because there would be no more milk but because they were very fond of the cow, as she was a sweet-natured old dear and they admired the way she could lick her

nostrils with her long tongue. What would they do for amusement when she was gone too?

The father put on his old jacket which had been bed and breakfast to generations of moths, cut a walking stick from the hedge and set off to follow the path over the mountain with the cow ambling along ahead of

him while she chewed her cud. The mountain was not very high and easily crossed. It was a short cut to the nearest town and he had travelled that familiar path many times in the past, admiring the view as he went, listening to the songbirds and keeping an eye out for berries and nuts. But with his brain buzzing because of all his worries that day, he was paying no attention to anything else at all, so it was some time before he realized that there was a very unusual silence all around him, as if everything natural was holding its breath. It was so very still and so very

quiet that you could hear an ant cough.
He stopped and the cow stopped.

He looked in puzzlement in every
direction but there was nothing to see
that could have made the world go so
quiet. When at last his gaze came back
to the place from where it had started,
namely, the back-end of the cow, he was
almost startled out of his boots to see

standing by the side of him, a strange little old man.

The little old man had glittering diamond-sharp eyes, and hair like boiled straw sticking out from under a big black pointed sort of hat. His face was without colour; even his lips were white. He had a nasty crooked sort of a smile showing teeth like a horse and he had a nose that was long and narrow and very tip-tilted at its end. He was wearing a big top coat that went from the ground right up to his chin, from where a few wiry hairs sprouted. This face was not at all attractive.

Mick stared at the stranger and because he was a happy-go-lucky sort of man, his first thought was a cheerful one: You could hang a bucket from the end of that nose!

His next thought was: How did he get so close without me seeing or hearing him? There is something very wrong about this!

Then fear struck him inside like a belt from a shovel and he trembled, thinking: He is not from this world and there is something about him that chills me to my soul.

As if he had read all of Mick's thoughts, the strange little old man glared at him in silence for a few moments with eyes that seemed to be reflecting fire, and then he asked: "Where are you taking the cow?"

The sound of his voice was like that of a crow suffering from the croup, most dreadfully harsh and rasping.

"I am taking her to the town, sir,"

Mick answered politely, but in a voice that quivered with his fear.

"Is she for sale?" the stranger asked.

"Indeed she is."

"I'll buy her if you'll sell her to me."

Now this was a hard choice for the poor man to make. He was terrified of the stranger and he did not want to

have anything to do with him in any way; but he was afraid to refuse him. What might this mysterious and horrifying little man do if he were denied the cow? Mick dreaded to think of it! The stranger might cast some kind of terrible spell or call down a curse on a man who was already in much trouble. The poor man's mind ran on these thoughts over and over again, until he said at last: "What price would you pay for her, sir?"

"I'll make a bargain with you," the little man said. "If you give me the cow, I'll give you this bottle." And with that

he pulled out a blue bottle from underneath his coat and held it up to the light. It was empty – just a blue bottle – it didn't even have a cork!

Well! This struck Mick as being very funny and despite being still very frightened, he laughed and laughed.

"Laugh if you must," the stranger

said, "but you'll never get a better price. This bottle is better than any money you could get at any market in the whole world, let alone in Ireland."

"Hard to believe," said Mick, who was still laughing. "And harder still to face my wife! To give my beautiful cow for a bottle? Molly would think I had a turnip on my shoulders instead of a head! And what about the rent? What would we do without money? The landlord would throw us out to live on the side of the road without a roof to shelter us."

He had stopped laughing.

"So you won't sell her to me?"

"No! Without disrespect, sir, I couldn't — not even for a bottle that was full with the best of wine — and with a cork in its neck to keep out the dust."

"Listen to me," said the stranger. "If you take this bottle you'll be a rich man — if you do not take it you will be a beggar all your life. I ask you for the last time, Mick Purcell!"

Mick was very shocked. How does he know my name? he wondered and he trembled even more.

The stranger continued: "Mick Purcell, I know you well and I have a

regard for you; therefore agree to this bargain or you may be sorry for it. And how do you know that your cow won't die before you ever have a chance to sell her? Why! She might not even take ten more steps. Don't throw away your luck, Mick Purcell!"

Suddenly Mick remembered the dear departed pig and the poor dead chickens of loving memory and a different kind of fear came into him. If the cow died suddenly he would have nothing at all, and per-haps the stranger would cast a bad spell on the cow out of spite if he

didn't get her. That cleared his mind considerably.

"I'll take the bottle," he said. "The cow is yours."

"You have made a good choice," the strange little man said. "Now listen carefully to what I tell you and do exactly as I say. When you

get home you mustn't mind if your wife is angry. Be calm and quiet and tell her to sweep the kitchen floor and put a clean cloth on the table. Then put the bottle on the ground and say these words: 'Bottle, bottle, do your duty', and then wait and see what will happen."

"And is that it?"

"It is! Except – do not let anyone outside of your family know anything at all about what has happened or will happen!"

"My wife will have forty fits – I know it!"

"She can have fifty fits if she likes! Do as I have said and all will be well," the strange little old man said. "Go home now!"

Mick turned for home, putting the bottle carefully inside his ragged old shirt next to his skin. There he could clutch it close to him and be sure that it was safe as he made his way back to the

cottage and his family.

He had only gone about six paces when he turned his head to have another look at the stranger. To his immense surprise the strange little old man and the cow were not to be seen; they had vanished from human sight.

"Merciful Heavens!" said Mick as he walked on. "May all that's good protect

me and my family!"

When he got home Molly was surprised that he was back so soon.

"I didn't expect you back for a long while yet! You didn't go over the mountain all the way to town and back again so quickly, did you? What happened? Did you sell the cow? How much money did you get? Can we pay the rent with a bit left over to start again?" The questions tumbled out of her mouth in a rapid flow, she was so full of excitement and curiosity.

"I sold the cow – for this!" said

the husband, holding up the bottle.

"What!?" screamed Molly, hitting High C without the slightest trouble. "What!?" she screamed again. She was wild with grief.

The little children huddled together for they had never seen their mother behave like this before.

"Listen, Molly dear!" said the husband and he tried to tell her the whole story, but she was in such a state that she scarcely listened to him; she kept cutting in with bitter remarks as he tried to explain. At one stage she said that if she lived for another thousand

years she wouldn't understand it!

And then she said: "What am I to do – boil that bottle with a handful of grass and a pinch of salt to make soup?"

The poor man, remembering that he had been instructed to be quiet and calm, said: "No – indeed not – just be patient with me and listen."

But she couldn't listen – not yet. She had to have her tuppence worth.

"Why didn't you use your brains? Have you no head at all?"

"I have a head," he answered mildly.

"You have a head – and so has a pin!" she responded tartly.

With that, she broke into tears.

The poor man comforted her and in a little while she calmed down and listened to what he had to say. At last she understood what had happened and the terrible position her husband had been in and she then asked his forgiveness. She dried her eyes and swept the kitchen floor until not a speck of dust

remained, and got out an ancient well-darned and patched white table-cloth — one that her grandmother had bought second-hand from a stall in a market many years before for threepence.

She took the table-cloth outside and shook it to get rid of its creases, gently so as not to cause it to rip as it was so fragile; and then she went back in, closing the front door behind her, and she spread the cloth on the table.

Feeling very nervous because he didn't know what would happen, Mick stood the bottle very carefully on the floor.

"Bottle, bottle, do your duty!" said he.

In a flash two small men leapt out of the bottle and in almost no time at all the table was covered with dishes and cutlery of silver and gold, laden with the most wonderful and delectable food. Then they flew back inside the bottle again. Zap! They were quicker than a sneeze! The small family barely had time to see them and they were totally astounded at what had happened.

After a few moments of staring at the bottle in a sort of stupor – it seemed to be as empty as before – they all turned their gaze to the table.

What a dinner was laid out for them there!

On the silver and golden dishes was a roasted goose whose stuffing had burst through its golden skin like a delicious lava, accompanied by a dish of apple sauce; there was a boiled chicken with its fragrant, mouth-watering soup, a

huge mound of floury potatoes, a great slab of butter and dishes of perfectly-cooked vegetables. A delightful aroma rose from these wonders in clouds of steam. There were silver goblets of good fresh milk and lemonade, and as well as all these delights there was a plum pie and a strawberry tart with small jugs of the thickest cream ever seen in this world. It was a feast, a banquet – and more than fit for any king.

At first they hesitated, afraid to touch anything in case it disappeared like the strange old man himself and the two who had gone back into the bottle.

They all knew then what the strange little old man was; and Mick, who had been afraid that he might be something worse, said: "The fairy man told the truth. God be praised!"

The children each had some of the chicken with a little of the potatoes and vegetables and a serving of the

nourishing soup. As the goose was very rich, far too rich really for people who had eaten frugally all their lives, the children were given only a small sliver each with a spoonful of apple sauce. Then young Billy chose to have a very little of the strawberry tart and small Ellen voted for the plum pie, each dressed gloriously in luscious cream. The smiles on their faces were something to behold!

Both parents found themselves unable to eat very much although they enjoyed every mouthful; and when they had all finished, they experienced the

strangest sensation they had ever felt —
they were all full up to bursting point —
and that was even without stuffing
themselves!

For a long while, filled with wonder,
they all talked about everything that
had happened. The sleepy and contented
children were at last put to bed and
Molly cleared the remaining food on to

their ordinary plates and put it in the bottom of her battered old dresser. Next, she carefully washed the gold and silver dishes while Mick dried them with nervous hands, using his best shirt, the one with only a few holes, as a drying cloth – they had nothing else that was good enough. Luckily it had been washed ready for Sunday and it smelled sweetly of the wild roses and honeysuckle that bloomed in the hedge where it had been spread to dry.

When that was done, they set the beautiful dishes back on the table, on top of the old white cloth which was

still miraculously clean. Not one grease-spot was on the cloth, not even where the little children had slurped their soup and had accidentally knocked bits of food off their plates.

Knowing that this had been the best night of their lives, they sat, one each side of the fire, watching the magic

bottle which was still in position on the floor, and they waited for the tiny men to leap out and take back their dishes. They waited and waited. It was well after one o' clock in the morning when they had to give in, they were so very sleepy, and go to bed.

In the morning they were surprised to find that the dishes were still where

they had left them. It began to dawn on them just what the fairy man had meant when he had said that they would be rich. They had enough food to last them several days and when that was all eaten, they tried the magic bottle again.

Just as before, the little men flashed out of the bottle, leaving a sumptuous meal and more of the silver and gold. It was true! The precious things were theirs!

Carrying the valuable dishes in a clean sack, the father set off for the town where he could sell them. This

time, he went the long way and did not use the path over the mountain. He came back driving a horse and cart that was their very own. The cart was piled high with things that were sorely needed – new beds and bedding, new clothes and many other things besides. In two lidded baskets, there was a dainty pink piglet and four pretty hens and sauntering along behind the cart with a halter round her neck was a red and white cow. The father had bought them not because they were needed but to please the children.

They were overjoyed.

The neighbours soon noticed how well-off the family had become, but no matter how many times they questioned as to where all the good fortune had come from, not one of the family would tell – even the little children. One neighbour, who had seen Mick drive his cow up the mountain path

and then come back down without the cow – too quickly to have gone very far – told all the others, and soon there was a great gang of people on the mountain, all driving their cows ahead of them, creating a terrible confusion and commotion with their pushing and shoving. They all hoped for some kind of good luck; but they hoped in vain. They did not begrudge the family their good fortune though, for no one went away from their door without good help. The best of food was given to all of them and money for the rent and other things.

Of course the landlord too noticed the family's new-found wealth. He agreed to let them have the use of some extra land for a higher rent, but he would not sell to them one inch of ground or the little cottage. The landlord was a hard-hearted man who had a quick false smile and the sly eye, and about as much compassion as a toffee-apple.

He pestered the family for a long, long time to find out their secret. In the end, Mick gave in and told him about the magic bottle.

"If you do not give me that bottle," said the landlord, "I'll boot you out of here!"

Mick gave the bottle to the landlord, thinking that as they were now so very

well-off, they wouldn't really need it any more.

It was the greatest mistake of his whole life.

In a short time they had the same disasters all over again and the money was soon gone. There was nothing for it but to sell the second cow and off Mick went with the cow ahead of him to walk the mountain path again, hoping to meet the strange little man once more.

And – it happened!

Just as before, there was the same stillness of sound and there was the same little man standing beside him.

"You're here again, are you, Mick Purcell? And with a cow to sell?"

"Yes, sir, I am, sir," the father answered very eagerly, his heart leaping with delight because of being lucky enough to meet the fairy man for a second time.

"I told you that you would be rich, did I not?"

"You did indeed and it was the truth. But I am not rich now as things have gone badly for me. Have you another bottle to swap? If you have, you are welcome to take my cow for it."

"Here is the bottle," the fairy man said, with an odd kind of smile. "You know what you must do with it – the same as before. You will never see me again so don't look for me. Turn for home now. Farewell for ever, Mick Purcell!"

Mick handed over the cow and went back down the mountain without once

looking back. He rushed into his house, yelling exultantly: "I have another bottle!"

"Oh! What lucky people we are!" cried Molly and she rushed about, sweeping like a gale, shaking the table-cloth, this time like a terrier with a rat, and setting it on the table.

As before, the father put the bottle on the floor and shouted out: "Bottle, bottle, do your duty!"

In a split second, two great brawny men with big sticks were out of the bottle and they were walloping and thumping and battering the husband

and wife around the kitchen until they were both too worn out to run any more and they lay down on the floor. The two brutes didn't touch the children at all, but they were wildly upset and crying.

Then little Billy shouted out: "Stop it! Stop it! Leave my mother and

father alone!"

Obeying instantly, the two muscular men shot back inside the bottle. How they fitted into it is anyone's guess.

Later on, when they had recovered somewhat, Mick sat thinking his thoughts. After some time he stood up, put the bottle under his jacket and set off to visit his landlord.

The landlord's house was ablaze with lights because he was having a party that night. Why not? He could well afford it! A servant went to tell him that one of his tenants was at the door.

"What do *you* want?" the landlord said rudely when he saw who it was.

"Nothing at all, sir. I have another bottle. I thought you'd like to know," Mick said politely.

"Is it as good as the first one?" The landlord's eyes were alight with greed.

"It's far better than the first one

and if you like I'll show it to you and all your friends."

"Come on in," said the landlord, showing Mick into a great hall where he saw his old bottle high up on a shelf.

"Now! Let us all see this new bottle and what it can do," the landlord said.

Mick set the bottle on the floor and he said the magic words.

In half a split second the two muscular brutes whizzed out of the bottle with even heavier cudgels in their hands. They pitched into the whole company and in moments there was uproar. The landlord was black

and blue on the floor; servants, ladies and gentlemen were screeching and running, shoving and pushing and trying to leg it out through the open doorway. But not one escaped. The two brawny men were leaping around as if they had invisible fireworks in their boots. They were everywhere at once, raining down blows and tumbling everybody and everything about.

The landlord got the worst of it. He was covered in bruises, gravy, custard and jelly; and he was yelling at the top of his voice.

"Stop them!" he shouted. "Stop

these demons ... or I'll have you arrested!"

"Not until I get my own bottle," Mick replied. "And if you threaten me again you'll get ten times more than you are getting now."

"Give him his bottle!" roared the landlord.

A servant scrambled to the shelf where the bottle stood and handed it down to Mick who put it safely inside his jacket.

As soon as he had done that, the two burly men leapt back inside the green bottle, and he picked that one up

too. Then he went home.

What a party there was in the little house that night, with all the neighbours invited! The little children from every house for miles around were deliriously happy – it was like having a hundred Christmas dinners in one go.

And afterwards?

The small mountain became known as Bottle Hill.

The landlord changed his ways — not wanting another visit from the tough men who lived in the second bottle; he became as mild as milk and twice as wholesome and as timid as a butterfly. And when Billy grew up to be a handsome man, he married the landlord's daughter. She was kind and beautiful beyond words. Mick, Molly and young Ellen went to live in the landlord's big house with Billy and his lovely wife.

Need it be said that they all lived long and happy lives?

And as to the bottles, what happened to them?

Certain people say that they were broken by some of the servants while having a fight; others think they were thrown out by mistake with the empties after one of their many jovial parties.

Perhaps they are still lying in a ditch somewhere in the south west of Ireland, waiting to be found by some lucky person.

It is possible, after all.